FIREWORKS IN THE NIGHT

FEATURING MUSIC BY HANDEL

Written by:
Sherry Miller

Illustrated by:
John M. Tatulli

FREE AUDIO DOWNLOAD AT *kidzjumpjamnjive.com*

Text copyright ©2015 by Sherry Miller TXu 1-963-353
Illustrations copyright ©2016 by John M. Tatulli
All right reserved, including the right of reproduction in whole or in part in any form.

Published by Kidz Jump Jam n' Jive Publishing a Division of S Music Studio LLC.
892 Port Penn Rd. Middletown, DE 19709
(302) 838-5330
www.kidzjumpjamnjive.com

ISBN 978-0-692-56696-1 Hardback
ISBN -13: 978-1523979844 Soft cover
Type was set in Curse Casual
The artwork was created digitally

"Water Music: Suite No. 1 in F Major, HWV 348: X. Allegro"
Composed By: Handel
Performed By: Prague Chamber Soloists, Andrew Mogrelia
Courtesy of Naxos of America

"Music for the Royal Fireworks, HWV 351: IV. La rejouissance"
Composed By: Handel
Performed By: Capella Istropolitana, Bohdan Warchal
Courtesy of Naxos of America

The Audio download accompanying Randy The Raccoon and His Musical Friends 'Fireworks in the Night' was recorded by Don Zabitka.
Narration and character voices by Sherry Miller, Forrust Miller, Larry Krebs, Hope Zabitka and Chris Duncan.

Hardcopy printed by IngramSparks ingramsparksupport@ingramcontent.com
Soft cover printed by Createspace an Amazon Company

"Handel is the greatest composer that ever lived. I would uncover my head and kneel on his grave." ~ Beethoven

Many thanks to my husband and daughters for their tireless encouragement, my friends who so graciously let me record their voices, my amazing illustrator and all of you yet to read this book. ~ Sherry

Dear Jacob,
I hope you enjoy my book.
Dream Big and Keep reading.
Sherry Miller
&
Randy

"Just wait until Farmer Heather sees this mess! Randy is in big trouble now."

"Horses, come on. Everyone in your stalls, it's dinner time!"

Stomp your feet,
clap your hands,
Let's join Randy and
the Rock a Note band.

Melody, Matty, Precious
too, Tug, Victoria, Sugar
and YOU.

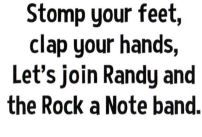

Stomp your feet,
clap your hands,
Let's join Randy and
the Rock a Note band.

Musical adventures
are so much fun,
Everything happens
when the day is done.

This is Randy, a very mischievous raccoon. He loves to pick through trash and play the piano.

On one of Randy's many adventures through the woods he discovered Rock a Note Farm, on Harmony Lane. This wasn't any ordinary farm. All the animals on the farm loved music as much as Randy.

Randy started joining the animals every night as they practiced their music. Randy fit in so well that farmer Heather asked him if he would like to live on the farm.

Randy was overjoyed that he finally had a home, and friends he could share stories with. One of the stories he loved to share was about his great, great, great, great, great grandpa, who he was named after, the legendary Randy the Bandit. He was one of the most wanted raccoons ever. The animals loved listening to Randy's stories.

"He stole banana peels and leftover peanut butter and jelly sandwiches right out of people's trash cans!"

"Wow, people must have been really scared of him." Snickered Sugar.

"Yeah, they were, but no one ever caught him in the act." Winked Randy

"Do you think he's still alive?" Asked Matty.

"All I know is there's still a reward out for his arrest. That's all I have time to tell you now…I'm gonna go pick through some trash."

When Randy wasn't telling stories about his famous relative, he entertained his friends with tales about the magical woods he had traveled through. The animals begged Randy to take them the next time he went on one of his adventures.

One night, when the moon was full and you could hear the frogs and crickets sing, Randy told the animals to get ready.

"Tonight's the night!" He said as he bounced up and down.

After everyone was fed, Farmer Heather hugged them all and said goodnight. The horses pretended to be asleep.
    "This is ridiculous." Tug grumbled.
    "I just know our plan will be discovered." Whispered Precious.
    "Will you two stop grumbling and close your eyes?" Scolded Victoria.

"Farmer Heather's asleep. It's time to rock n' roll!"

Suddenly, the animals came to the edge of the woods and found themselves surrounded by crowds of people. It looked like a costume party.

"Where are we?" Asked Tug.

"It looks like a pah-taaaaay." Randy said excitedly.

"This doesn't feel right." Said Precious

"Look over there. That poster hanging on the tree looks just like you, Randy." Matty said pointing to the sign.

"Wow, that really does look like me. I wonder if that's my great, great, great, great, great grandpa, Randy the Bandit?" Randy said.

"I knew we shouldn't have come." Cried Precious.
"This could mean trouble." Neighed Sugar.

"No way! I don't know about you guys but I'm going to find out what the celebration is all about." Chattered Randy.

"Well, we can't let him go alone." Said Matty and Melody.
"I don't have a problem letting him go alone." Sugar said.

"Come on you guys, we started together so I guess we'll stick together, too." Commanded Tug.

As the animals reluctantly enter the crowd, people stared at them as they passed.
   "What are they looking at? You would think they had never seen animals before." Victoria snorted.

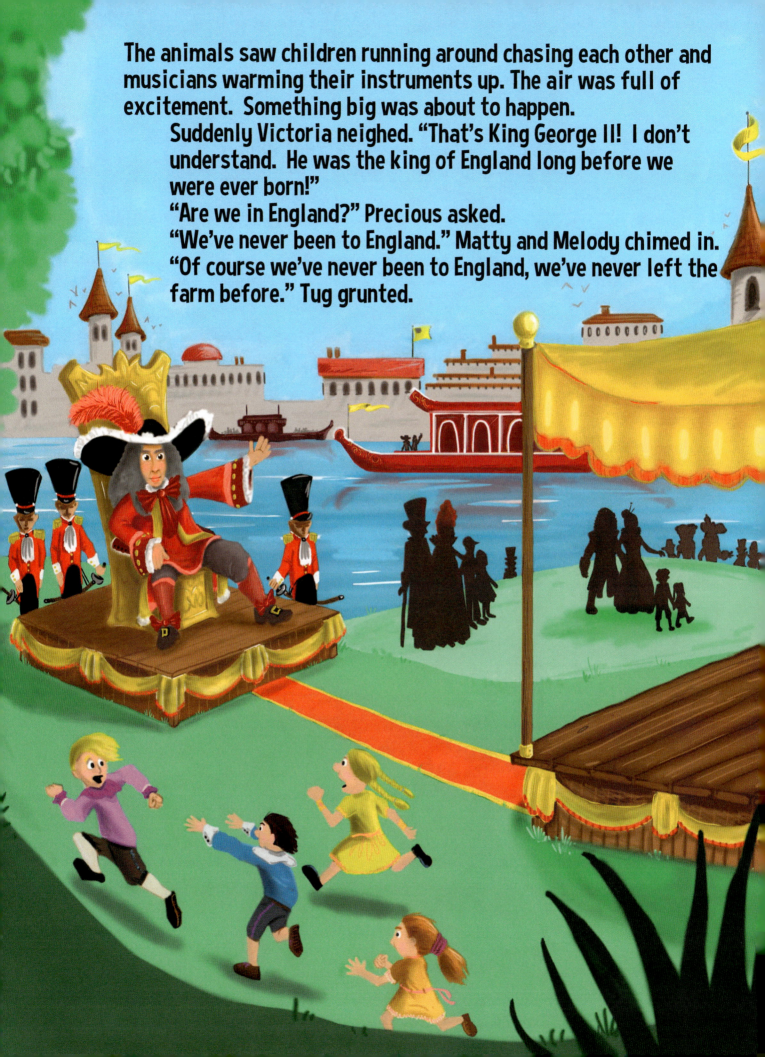

The animals saw children running around chasing each other and musicians warming their instruments up. The air was full of excitement. Something big was about to happen.

Suddenly Victoria neighed. "That's King George II! I don't understand. He was the king of England long before we were ever born!"

"Are we in England?" Precious asked.

"We've never been to England." Matty and Melody chimed in.

"Of course we've never been to England, we've never left the farm before." Tug grunted.

"I told you the woods were Magical."
Randy said with a twinkle in his eye.

The King of England asked George Frideric Handel, a German musician, to write some music to be played at his big fireworks display. Thousands of people came to watch the fireworks and hear 100 musicians play Handel's music. The music that Handel wrote was so wonderful that people thought it was better than the fireworks! Listen and see if you can hear the trumpets? They play a very important part in this music. Trumpets are part of the brass family.

Little did the animals know that while they were listening to the music something bad was about to happen. Actually, two bad things were about to happen.

The song you are listening to is "Water Music",
the piece that Handel wrote to be played on a big floating boat.

Anyway back to our story.

While the animals watched the fireworks and listened to the beautiful music they saw one of the fireworks go sideways instead of up. Oh no!! The firework hit the stage where the musicians were playing and started a fire. The musicians grabbed their instruments and ran, while people in the crowd screamed and scattered. This show was turning out to be as exciting as any rock concert Randy had ever been to.

As he looked around he couldn't help but notice that a group of people were starting to whisper to each other and point in his direction. Something just didn't feel right. Before Randy could turn around a guard stepped in front of him.

"Halt! You with the black and white striped suit." Said a guard pointing his sword at Randy.

"We finally caught you, Randy the Bandit. You won't escape now."

If the fire on the stage wasn't enough, now a guard had mistaken Randy for his great, great, great, great, great grandpa, Randy the Bandit. What was he going to do? The animals didn't know what was happening, but they knew they had to get Randy out of there. Tug reared and began to gallop full force towards the guard.

"Hop on!" He neighed, as he galloped towards Randy. Randy jumped, and grabbed Tug's tail as he sped by, hanging on for dear life.

"Go Tug, go!" Randy cried.

They could hear people shouting behind them making Tug gallop even faster. Tug remembered his days on the racetrack and headed towards the woods at a full gallop. Randy almost fell off several times as Tug swerved around trees and jumped over fallen logs in the way.

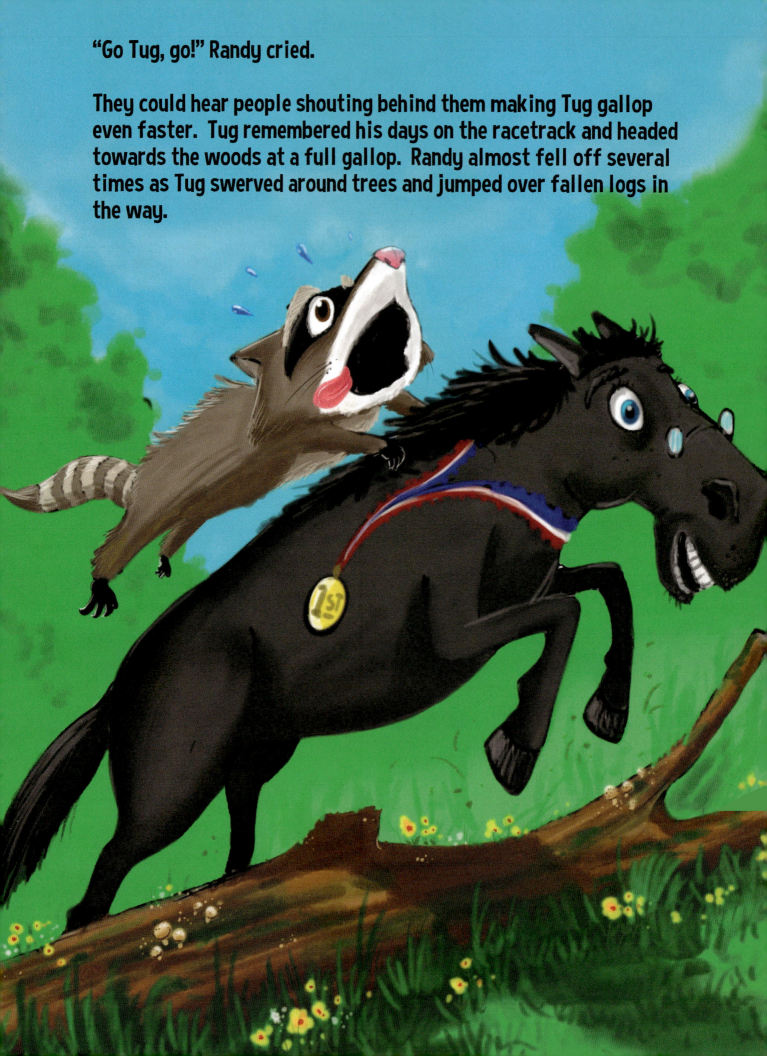

Finally, Tug slowed down. They could no longer hear the crowd. It was quiet again.
"Where was everyone?" Tug stopped and turned to look behind him.
"Did the others escape, too?" Tug and Randy wondered.

Just when they thought that their friends might not have made it out, they heard Victoria whinny and saw Sugar trot into view with Melody and Matty on her back.

Boy were they glad to see all their friends.

"Thanks Tug. You're the best friend a raccoon like me could ever ask for."
"It was nothing, Randy. That's what friends do."

"Thanks for taking us on that adventure, Randy. Even though I was scared, I still had lots of fun." Said Precious, smiling.
"You're getting all sappy on me. Cut it out!" Snapped Sugar.
"We think it's sweet." Melody and Matty purred.

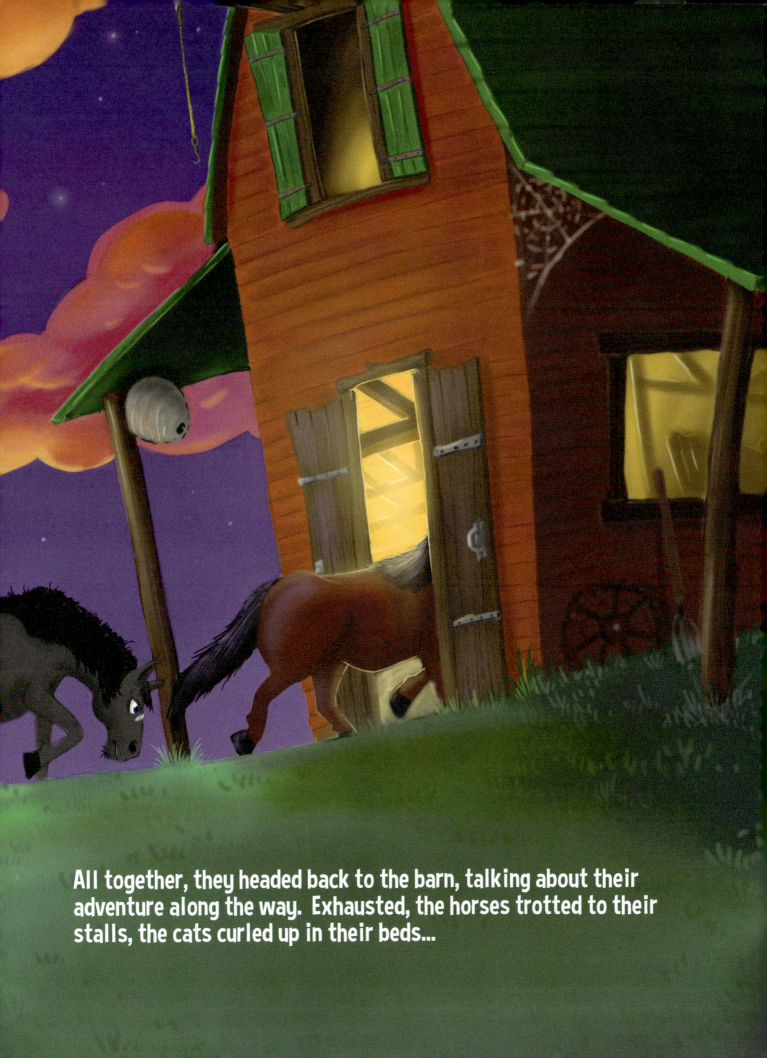

All together, they headed back to the barn, talking about their adventure along the way. Exhausted, the horses trotted to their stalls, the cats curled up in their beds...

and Randy found his favorite warm spot in the hayloft. He smiled as he drifted off to sleep, dreaming of 100 musicians playing music to the booming sounds of fireworks.

THE END

FUN FACTS ABOUT GEORGE FRIDERIC HANDEL

1. Handel was born in Germany but moved to England when he was 27. That's where he met King George II.

2. Handel's father wanted him to become a lawyer and wouldn't let him study music. One of his relatives gave him a clavichord (a type of piano) that he hid in the attic. He would practice in secret after his father went to bed.

3. Over 12,000 people gathered to hear the performance of "Music for the Royal Fireworks", causing a 3 hour traffic jam on the London Bridge. The people really liked Handel's music.

4. Handel's father was a barber-surgeon. How would you like someone who cut your hair also operating on you? That's how they did it back then.

5. The men wore wigs to be fashionable. But it all started with King Louis XIII who went bald early in life. To cover up his head he started wearing a wig. To keep the wigs from smelling they would put powder on them. They were called powdered wigs.

6. Handel wrote the famous "Messiah", which is performed both at Christmas and Easter. When King George II heard one of the songs called the "Hallelujah Chorus", he was so overwhelmed that he stood up. Now everyone stands when they hear the "Hallelujah Chorus".

After reading "Fireworks in the Night", you may be interested in listening to "Music for the Royal Fireworks", "Water Music" and "The Hallelujah Chorus" from The Messiah. These compositions and others by Handel can be found on YouTube.

I HOPE YOU'VE ENJOYED THE FIRST BOOK IN THIS SERIES ABOUT FAMOUS COMPOSERS. YOUR FEEDBACK IS SO IMPORTANT. PLEASE GO TO AMAZON AND GIVE US A REVIEW.

Made in the USA
Charleston, SC
04 April 2016